EVOCATIONS

Stories of Ghosts, Lovers, Karma and Paradise

Richard Howard

DEDICATED
to my very good friend

KEVIN WAITE

in gratitude for all his
kindness, encouragement
and practical help in
bringing to fruition
many of my writing projects

****

And
Special Thanks
to

MONIQUE OTAI

and

MICHAEL LISLE DUNN

CONTENTS

HAUNTED

It was quite by chance that I found myself where I was that day. I was staying as a guest with friends in the country, and because my host knew of my interest in ghosts and hauntings, he thought I'd be curious to see the place in question. He'd said nothing about where we were going as we set off, so I just assumed he was showing me the surrounding countryside. We chatted as he drove, catching up on our news, until eventually he pulled into a layby and I realised we were close to the entrance of a cemetery. In many ways I wish he'd never taken me there because there was something about the place that unnerved me. I didn't say so at the time but I was slightly surprised by my reaction. I'd investigated several strange places over the years and wasn't easily scared. But this was different.

We got out of the car, walked to the lychgate and entered the cemetery. I looked at my friend quizzically. He responded to the question he saw in my face.

"That church is haunted," he said casually.

Despite my unease, my interest was immediately engaged as we stood silently looking at a small church situated among the tombstones. It was an unremarkable building with no distinguishing features, a place I might never have noticed without it being drawn to my attention.

"Haunted? How?" I asked.

"For some years, people have said they hear the organ playing when the church is locked at night, and some have reported seeing an eerie light moving about inside, illuminating the stained glass window by the tower."

It was an intriguing description and I wondered what music

was played. Was it something recognisable? Hymns? Bach? Or simply some ghostly dirge of minor chords as if a dead hand lay across the keyboard?

"It's all hearsay, of course," he continued, "but I'm struck by the number of times people have mentioned it since we moved here. So I thought you'd be interested."

"I am," I said with slight reluctance, as my disquiet persisted.

"Shall we go inside?" he suggested.

Walking the short distance to the main door, we passed between large and elaborate Victorian tombs, overgrown, crumbling, grandiose and neglected, incongruously surrounded by neatly trimmed grass beyond which, in the far distance, were more recent headstones in the part of the cemetery still in use.

Arriving at the porch, I went ahead and lifted the rusty latch. The heavy door groaned on unoiled hinges and we were greeted with a cold mustiness as we stepped onto the tiled floor within. My friend closed the door behind us and we stood motionless for a moment in the hollow silence. It was a chilled atmosphere in more ways than one. Was it the church? Or was it me? Like many an old country church, its ancient radiators were barely warm and the sunlight streaming in through stained glass threw cold, indifferent colours on the stone floor. I shivered.

"You all right?" my friend asked.

I reassured him as I looked up at the organ loft, wondering whether I'd dare to come here alone at night. What was it that possessed me? This unnerving feeling I'd never known before. I was certainly intrigued by the place and I think that was the very moment my haunting began.

Once back in the car, the feeling stayed with me, as if we took with us some essence of that strange place or had been joined by an invisible companion. More than once on our homeward journey, I felt compelled to look round and reassure myself there was no one sitting in the back seat. My friend, sensing my discomfort, asked again if I was all right. Naturally, I told him I was and tried to dismiss my increasing sense of dread.

Lying in bed that night, I realised I was not all right. Far from it. I'd slept well all week in the guest bedroom and was normally a sound sleeper, anyway, but I was restless and woke several times for no apparent reason. And once awake, all I could think about was that old church surrounded by tombs.

Fortunately, that was the last day with my friends and I must say I was glad to be leaving and travelling home to London. It had nothing to do with their excellent hospitality. My hosts were most gracious and had plainly been completely unaware of any change in atmosphere, though I think they noticed a change in me.

Travelling home, the train was crowded and would become more so as we approached London. I was fortunate to secure a seat in a compartment already occupied by five others. At the next station we were joined by a man who sat next to me, leaving just one seat vacant, the one opposite me. At the following station people boarded the train searching for a seat. Several looked into our compartment but then moved on, plainly thinking it was full. In an effort to be helpful, I half rose from my seat, pointing at the one opposite to indicate that it wasn't occupied, at which point everyone in the compartment looked at me in a very odd way and the man next to the vacant seat glanced in its direction and smiled. That's when the truth dawned. Sitting opposite, following and watching me, was someone visible to everyone else except me. I felt foolish ~ and afraid.

Eventually, arriving at my flat, I let myself in the communal door and noticed straight away that it didn't close as quickly as it usually did. Glancing back, I saw it poised half open and motionless before finally springing closed as if someone else had entered behind me.

Away from the obligations of being a congenial house guest and the subsequent pressure of the crowded train, I sat back in my armchair to relax with a drink and take stock. A sense of relief soon came over me and for a moment everything felt completely normal. Being alone was never in itself a difficulty for me and was certainly preferable to being in the wrong company. But I was still preoccupied with the sensations I'd had ever since leaving the cemetery. Perhaps the pressure of being away from my own territory had begun to tell on me, making me uncomfortable, restless and prone to heightened imagination, a state that had continued to possess me until I was finally back in my own home. Being sociable for a week with friends certainly has its pleasures, but it still requires effort which, after a while, can begin to sap one's energy.

I thought about the door in the lobby, ten minutes previously, not closing behind me as it normally did. It seemed ludicrous that the strange feelings I'd had on that last day and night with my friends would persist all the way back to London. Surely it was just my tired imagination. Perhaps the simple explanation was that the spring mechanism of the door needed oiling. But I was less able to dismiss the incident on the crowded train. Plainly everyone could see that the seat opposite me was occupied, but I'm convinced it wasn't. How can I have sat there the entire journey unable to see directly in front of me what everyone else apparently could? Imagination is more likely to conjure things that aren't there. I've never heard that it can act in the opposite way and render invisible what *is* there.

As I tried to rationalise these thoughts, a sudden chill crept over me when I noticed a distinct depression in the cushions of the armchair that faced me ~ exactly as they would be if someone were sitting there. I leapt up and stood before the chair.

"Who are you?" I shouted.

In the ensuing silence, I felt my skin crawl. I didn't dare reach out for fear of what I might find myself touching. Slowly, as I watched, the cushions resumed their normal shape as if someone had stood up and walked away.

Unease consumed me for the rest of the evening. I succumbed to nervous restlessness in whatever I attempted to do until weariness overcame me and eventually it was time to sleep. But how could I sleep knowing there was someone or something in my flat? What if it attacked me when I was off guard during the night? I tried to calm myself through reason. It didn't have to wait for darkness to attack me, assuming that was its intention. It had the constant advantage of being invisible. If it was going to harm me in any way, surely it would have done so by now. Then I thought again of the incident on the train and wondered precisely what my fellow-passengers had seen sitting opposite me. Anything grotesque and I'd have seen it in their reactions. Surely it can only have been some perfectly normal, inconspicuous person of little or no consequence. Was it a man or a woman? But who? And what did they look like?

The next I knew, it was daylight. I must have exhausted myself with endless speculation and, to my relief and astonishment, had slept through the night. Sitting on the edge of my bed, just for a moment I completely forgot my fears. But not for long. A moment later I heard the sound of running water coming from the bathroom. Instantly I raced to see what was happening. In the few seconds it took me to reach the bathroom door, the sound stopped. I flung the door open. There was no running water, no water in either the bath or the washbasin, but the room was full of steam. I waited for it to clear before cautiously going in. Then, rinsing my hands at the washbasin, I glanced up at the mirror in front of me and froze. Three letters were written in the steam: RLS.

During breakfast, insofar as I had any appetite at all, I couldn't help looking around for evidence of my invisible stalker, but soon gave up and tried to focus on what I was doing. What was the point of wearing myself out trying to see something that refused to reveal itself? Although I couldn't help thinking of it as 'it', I had to remind myself that I was probably dealing with a person and the initials on the mirror seemed to confirm this.

Was it an answer to my question of the previous night when I yelled 'Who are you'? If it was, I was none the wiser as the letters meant nothing to me. It seemed to be an attempt at communication. But why? And why with me? I had little time to wonder about it any longer as I had to be at my office within the hour. Hastily I finished my coffee, showered, dressed and left the flat. As I went downstairs to the lobby, I met a neighbour at the foot of the stairs who smiled and waited for me to pass. When I glanced back, I saw he was still waiting as if there was a second person coming down behind me.

Strange as it might seem, I found myself becoming accustomed to these odd moments that suggested others were able to see someone that I couldn't. I could have asked my neighbour who or what he saw coming down the stairs behind me, but decided against it since, at best, it would make me seem very odd, and at worst, perhaps a little mad. Then out of curiosity, I wondered how my work colleagues would respond to a stranger in their midst.

Once in my office, I was continually aware of the same presence close by as I waited for others to react. But no one did, which suggested to me that whoever was following my every move, could choose whether others saw him or not. So why didn't he reveal himself to me? One thing I did notice, however, was that my work colleagues seemed to avoid me that day. I'm sure I didn't imagine it. Normally there would at least be some passing conversation but whenever I stepped from my office to make coffee in the kitchen, others left the room with only the barest acknowledgement of me, and as I passed desks in the open plan office, all eyes were turned away. What was it they sensed about me that made me feel I was being ostracised? It was difficult not to feel paranoid. Does one have a choice about feeling paranoid?

That night my sleep was disturbed by the most vivid dream. I was back in the cemetery. One minute it was daylight, the next I was plunged into darkness. The church was silhouetted by the moon and the ancient tombs glowed with an unearthly light. Wandering aimlessly between endless rows of graves, having to feel my way in impenetrable darkness, I recoiled several times as my groping hands touched bones covered with slime. Whenever I saw a way out and hastened towards it, the scene immediately changed and I was presented with a new vista of endless tombs stretching even deeper into darkness. Unable to see more than a few feet in front of my face, a screaming figure leapt from a sarcophagus, enveloping me in blackness and I woke trembling with fear.

Throwing off the duvet, I was relieved to be back in the real world. But my relief was short lived when I saw, standing in the darkest corner of my bedroom, a tall, gaunt figure staring at me with accusing eyes. There was no face, just the eyes and the faintest outline of a man who then turned away and disappeared into shadow. Like a frightened child, I hugged the duvet tightly around me and buried my face in the pillows.

It was some while before I found the courage to get up and switch on every light in the flat, staggering to the armchair in the lounge to spend the rest of the night fitfully awake and alert for any further surprises. The shock of seeing the apparition in my room made dream and reality seem intricately connected. I had recently dared to hope that whoever had attached himself to me was relatively benign. After all, I had seen what I assumed were his initials, but now I felt compelled to believe in a far darker motive. Who was RLS?

After another week of continuing nightmares, I concluded that the only way to find answers, and hopefully lay to rest this increasingly terrifying experience, was to return to the cemetery. This time I wouldn't stay with friends. I'd hire a car, book a hotel and go alone. I had to face whatever awaited me.

After a four hour drive, convinced I was not alone, I arrived at the hotel by early afternoon, unpacked and took a shower. An hour later, armed with a map, the weather was fair as I set off to find the cemetery, only a ten minute drive away. Parking in the same layby as before, I felt the same sense of foreboding and hesitated before getting out of the car. But the longer I sat there, the more uncomfortable I became. Eventually I was compelled by my invisible tormentor to do whatever it was I'd come to do.

Passing beyond the lychgate, a sense of doom descended on me but I was at a loss to know exactly what I should do next. I wondered if my decision to return had been too rash, while another part of me reasoned it was the most likely way to rid myself of whoever was haunting me. Although it was only the second time I'd set foot in the place, seeing those ancient tombs I felt an unwelcome sense of familiarity, rekindling my horrific dream of several nights before. Walking nervously between them,

I noticed they were not only crumbling but, in some, chunks of stone had fallen away, allowing glimpses of the rotting darkness within. It was from one of these that I remembered vividly the shadowy figure of my nightmare springing out to engulf me in its black world. The afternoon sunlight did nothing to weaken the memory.

Leaving those dark, forbidding tombs, I wandered across the lawn towards the newer part of the cemetery, more tranquil and less hemmed in, where headstones were legible, each one hinting at its owner's individual story. Strolling through churchyards was something I'd done many times over the years, not least because they were quiet places of contemplation away from everyday problems. How often I'd stood before a grave wondering how or why the occupant had died so young or what events an aged person had lived through. While some inscriptions betrayed the yearning of the bereaved, other seemed trite or matter of fact: 'rest in peace', 'sleeping', 'gone to Jesus'. But I knew that many were neither asleep nor at peace. My experiences in psychic investigation were testament to that, not to mention the unnerving events of the past two weeks.

As I wandered between row upon row of headstones, my attention was suddenly drawn to one in particular. Why, I wasn't sure, since the stone itself was very plain. Perhaps that's precisely what made it stand out amid the more elaborately carved and polished headstones surrounding it. Suddenly I felt as if I'd been prompted, led there, compelled to stop and read this particular inscription. And, as I did, a curious feeling crept over me. "Here lies Roger Le Strange, aged 22, a gifted and promising composer, unrecognised and unfulfilled, a life cut tragically short. 1916-1938" Was this RLS? It wasn't only the initials that caused that odd feeling in me, but something else. In that moment, a vague and distant memory came to me as if revealed by a sudden parting of clouds. I knew him.

I hadn't thought of Roger Le Strange for years. Our paths had crossed decades before, then we lost touch and I had no idea what became of him. As I said at the beginning, it was quite by chance

I'd found myself there that afternoon with my friend, and I was completely unaware it was where RLS ended his short life. A wave of emotion swept over me at the thought of his demise, which felt odd and inappropriate, since our acquaintance had been so brief.

Back at the hotel, I was pursued by the same persistent presence wherever I went. After dinner, I loitered in the lobby, reluctant to go back to my room. I picked up some brochures about the local village and their history and read them with a drink in the bar. Eventually returning to my room, I felt increasingly irritated at the thought of being hounded by someone I'd barely known. Shutting the door behind me, I swung round to confront the empty space that I now believed to be Roger Le Strange.

"What do you want?" I shouted.

In the silence that followed, I wondered for the first time if I was going mad. No, I was being driven mad by someone too cowardly to show himself. But why?

That night I dreamt again. It was night and raining. I wandered down a dark street. A lamp illuminated the far end. As I approached, I saw a youth, drenched and filthy, slumped against the lamp post, only half conscious. I went to help him. As I reached down, he looked up at me and smiled. A moment later I was looking into the empty eye sockets of a skull. I recoiled in panic as the skull floated upwards beyond my reach, staring at me as it disappeared into the night. I turned away, looking back at the street I'd just walked down. The houses that had been there were now tombs and I was alone in a cemetery.

I woke startled, unsure where I was. Panicking, I reached out, found the bedside light and realised I was in my hotel room. It was still dark. I looked at my watch: four o'clock. As I lay wide awake, I was sure I heard movements in the room, then a rustling sound and heavy breathing too close for comfort. As I leapt from the bed everything was still and silent.

Haunted by my dream, I tried to remember anything I could about Roger Le Strange, but everything was blank. He was a passing acquaintance of little or no consequence. I hadn't remembered he was a composer until I read the inscription on his tombstone but I did wonder whether it was he who played the church organ at night. It seemed a logical assumption. A restless composer unable to move on from this world for whatever reason, might find solace in being able to commune with music. I knew many cases of earthbound spirits unable to leave this world after death because of some attachment or unfinished business that held them here. To the uninitiated, this explanation for hauntings is scoffed at and derided, but these are usually people who have no time at all for the prospect of any kind of life after physical death. My own investigations over many years convinced me that these cases are genuine and can be proven. Then I realised that if I wanted to confront my pursuer, perhaps I should be present when he plays the church organ.

And so it was decided. I would conceal myself in the church so as not to be found when it was locked up for the night. When I first visited the place with my friend, I was so unnerved that I would never have contemplated such a nocturnal vigil, but now I felt there was no other choice.

I returned to the cemetery the following day not long before dusk and wandered again past the grave of Roger Le Strange. Then I went back to the church, letting myself in as quietly as those creaking hinges would allow. It was empty and I looked around for a place to conceal myself. In a far corner, I discovered a tiny room where mops and brooms were kept along with various cleaning materials. It was the perfect place to hide. I couldn't imagine the sexton bothering to look there as he performed his nightly ritual of securing the church. As I checked my watch, I heard the familiar creak of the main door. I held my breath at the sound of footsteps. The sexton took a cursory glance to assure himself no one was there. He called out to make quite sure, paused a moment, and in the silence that followed, I heard retreating footsteps, the echoing bang of the heavy door and the clank of the key in the lock.

I decided to stay where I was for a while in case, still in the vicinity, he might sense my intrusion. I waited almost half an hour and during that time, wondered whether I would witness any psychic activity at all. In my experience, most hauntings were occasional, random and intermittent, perhaps coinciding with an anniversary of some kind, but there was no reliable pattern. Patience was a prerequisite for any psychic investigator but since this haunting seemed decidedly personal, I wondered if my presence would act as a catalyst.

Venturing from concealment, my eyes accustomed to the dark, I walked slowly along the nave to a spot from where I could see the organ loft and made myself as comfortable as I could, sitting on prayer cushions at the far end of a pew where, with my back against the wall, I had a perfect view of the organ. Now all I had to do was wait.

I was accustomed to waiting in such circumstances and used the time to analyse and reflect on memories of previous investigations, which one day I hoped to collate for publication. It always surprised me how much I could see in the dark once my eyes had adjusted and now, sitting where I was, my vision was aided by faint moonlight filtering through the stained glass, tinting everything with a subdued glow. Perhaps I nodded off for a few seconds but I was suddenly wide awake to the sound of a deep and solemn low chord on the organ. Looking up, I saw at the keyboard, a gaunt figure with his back to me. As a yearning melody unfolded, I realised I had heard this music before.

I was taken back three decades. The tune was painfully beautiful but I didn't want to hear it then or now. I covered my ears as supressed memories began to seep into my brain. I remembered a room with bare floorboards, a few items of crude furniture and an upright piano on which, with his back to me, Roger Le Strange was playing the same music. I remembered him telling me it was a piece he had just composed, the first part of a much larger work he had been inspired to write, having heard it in a dream. Even at his young age, he saw it as his magnum opus. But I didn't want to know. At that time, music was everything to me and I'd always harboured a secret desire to compose something myself. I never told him or anyone else about my ambition for fear of being ridiculed but as he continued playing, I was consumed with jealousy. I hid my feelings as best I could. Here was a young stranger I'd met by chance only a few weeks earlier, devoted to music, trusting me with his innermost creative thoughts in an act of friendship and to seek my opinion, and all I could feel was jealousy and anger.

In the dimly lit church, as the music continued, I fought desperately to deny and expel those unbearably painful memories which, until now, I had successfully supressed. Then, even as the music continued to play, Roger Le Strange was standing directly in front of me. With my back pressed to the church wall, desperate to retreat, I was forced to stare back at his young face. As he smiled, I instantly remembered my most despicable act.

Back in his sparsely furnished room, he finished playing and as I was about to leave, turned to me, reluctant and embarrassed, to tell me of his misfortune. Afflicted with a grave illness and unable to pay his rent, he had been ordered to leave. He had nowhere to go, no one else to ask, and would lose his most treasured piano if he couldn't find help. He didn't ask me to accommodate him, instead he asked for a loan that he would pay back as soon as he was established somewhere and could complete the work he was composing ~ a work of extraordinary pathos and beauty. Although we had been acquainted only a few weeks, I could so easily have helped him. But I chose not to. I denied him and, in so doing, robbed him of his dream to give the world this extraordinarily beautiful music. I never saw him again.

As he stood before me in the church, that act of denial tore at my conscience, consuming me with guilt. Simultaneously, I was acutely conscious that, devoid of any such talent, I had failed miserably to realise my own ambition to write music. Born out of pure jealousy, my mean-spirited, despicable response to his hesitant but most urgent plea, robbed him of all opportunity and abandoned him to his fate. Yet now he was smiling at me, just as the destitute young man in my dream had smiled when he gazed up at me from the ground. That was the fate of Roger Le Strange and it was the same smile. A smile of pity.

The organ continued to play ~ I have no idea how ~ as he turned to leave. By reminding me of that music, he had forced me to acknowledge memories I had successfully supressed for decades because I couldn't bear to admit to actions of which I was now deeply ashamed. The walls of my subconscious had been breached and everything I'd banished and denied poured in to take root in my consciousness.

As I've said before, it was quite by chance that I'd been taken to the cemetery where he was buried. Perhaps he sensed or recognised me and saw an opportunity to help me know myself better. Now he had confronted me in person, I knew he would no longer haunt me. Instead I would be haunted eternally by my own guilt and shame.

A year or so later, I heard from my friend that there had been no more reports of the organ playing at night. Perhaps Roger Le Strange had now moved on and found peace. I sincerely hope so and I wish him well.

MEMORIES

What if, when you woke up one morning, you knew this was the day you were going to die? How differently might you live that day? But not knowing might be a saving grace; not just because it would spare you the anxiety, but because it meant that fate would take its course in its own intended way. When Mark got out of bed that morning, as fit and healthy as ever, he had no idea that this was the day.

It was a Saturday. No need to rush to work. Instead there was plenty of time to linger over breakfast and decide what to do after the previous evening's boozy celebration of a friend's engagement. The friend in question had met his soon-to-be wife at the same time that Mark had met the love of his life. They were all at the same party several years previously and Mark had begun dating the girl called Yasmin almost immediately afterwards. It had been a passionate but complicated liaison ~ both of them were in other relationships at the time ~ and neither he nor she could bring themselves to face destroying what they already had with other partners. As a result, their affair couldn't survive and was only terminated when Yasmin and her husband moved away and all contact between Mark and herself was severed. At the time, painful as it was, they both thought it was for the best. Ironically, not long afterwards, Mark's partner ended their relationship because she had fallen in love with someone else. Subsequently, Mark had had a few on-off relationships but didn't seem able to find the right woman and so they had all petered out.

When the summer sun finally beamed into the kitchen where he sat and roused him from his reverie, he decided it was far too nice a day to stay at home. There were books he needed to return to the library and so as soon as breakfast was finished and he'd taken a shower, he headed there to dispose of several that were now overdue. And that was when it happened. He was just turning away from the counter when he was sure he'd seen Yasmin ~ or someone very like her ~ disappear between two rows of bookshelves. For a moment he was caught between excitement and reservation. What if she wasn't alone? His heart pounded and he caught his breath. A moment later he was standing between the two rows of shelves, desperate to confirm what he'd seen, but the only person there was an elderly man engrossed in a book. Quickly, Mark walked the length of the shelves to the bookcases that stood against the wall at the far end. The woman he'd seen would be browsing in the alcove and she must be there because there was no other way out.

Arriving at the shelves, he looked in both directions but there was no one. Disappointment verged on irritation as he noted the sign indicating the subject-matter of the books in front of him: *BEREAVEMENT*. He was sure ~ no, he knew ~ that he'd seen a woman who looked very like Yasmin, just as he remembered her, walk between the two rows of shelves that led to where he was now standing. Turning away, he sighed impatiently as he brushed past the elderly man still engrossed in his book and retraced his steps, looking expectantly in every direction. He searched every area of the library ~ from *GARDENING* via *TRAVEL* and *VISUAL ARTS* to *CONTEMPORARY FICTION* ~ but to no avail. The tension between excitement and frustration disorientated him and seeing a chair nearby, he sat down.

He stared at the floor in confusion and wondered what was happening. Was it celebrating his friend's engagement the previous night? Was it the memory of the two of them all those years ago meeting their respective girlfriends which was now dredging up painful feelings of his own eventual disappointment? Yasmin had certainly been the love of his life and somewhere deep inside, he felt sure that this was why he'd never managed to maintain subsequent relationships for very long. Absurd as it seemed, despite her moving away and cutting all ties, he realised that perhaps he still grieved for her. Was that why the notice above the books had so irritated him? Thinking he'd seen her in the library must have been a trick of his mind, especially as she looked just as he remembered her from years before. She would surely have changed by now and so it could only have been hallucination. Reluctantly, he left the library and headed for his favourite coffee shop.

Sitting by the window, gazing out at the passing traffic and Saturday morning shoppers, he distractedly sipped his coffee, plunged into vivid memories of his affair with Yasmin, which had lasted for more than a year before the pain became too much for either of them to bear. Neither had wanted to end it and yet the guilt and deceit on both sides became intolerable and they were forced to tear themselves apart. Then, as he glanced up, suddenly there she was again in the crowd. He was sure he had glimpsed her strolling past and his whole body tensed. Was she alone? He couldn't tell ~ and then she was gone.

Taking a final gulp of coffee, he fled the table, rushed through the shop and pushed past several people coming in through the door. Once on the street, he jostled his way through the crowd, desperate to catch up. She hadn't been walking quickly but she could be anywhere. Maybe she went into a shop. He craned to see ahead, stepping into the road to bypass the crowd which seemed intent on thwarting him. Then he thought he saw her strolling ahead of him. He hastened his step, half running but was then blocked by others who also stepped into the road. Almost in panic, he pushed past them as he moved closer. He recognised her walk, the back of her neck, her hairstyle. And she was alone, which gave him the confidence to approach. Then she stopped to look in a jeweller's shop window. Now was his chance. He pushed through the slow-moving crowd until finally he stood beside her. She glanced up at him and walked away. It wasn't her.

His heart raced with the effort, the hope, the expectation, but disappointment plunged him into depression as he watched her merge once more with the crowd. From the back, she still looked like Yasmin, which tormented him, even though he knew it wasn't her. He berated himself for being so foolish. So many women had a similar hairstyle, a similar walk, a similar presence. He had to let this go. But that didn't explain the incident in the library, where he was sure he'd seen a woman who looked just like her, disappear between two rows of bookshelves that led only to an area from which there was no exit. He remembered again the sign above the books: *BEREAVEMENT*. Could that really be what he was still feeling after five years? Could it conceivably have been reignited by celebrating his friend's engagement? It all seemed so unlikely, yet it didn't alter that fact that he was now plagued by images of his lost love.

To escape the crowd, he walked to a nearby park and settled himself on one of several available seats overlooking a pond. It was peaceful there and he needed to soothe his reeling thoughts and emotions. The sun warmed him and the sight of a pair of ducks paddling by on the calm water helped him relax. But the image of Yasmin still haunted him. He hadn't consciously thought about her for years, yet now she was so vivid in his mind. He could see her laughing, tossing back her head as she did so. He conjured a dozen treasured moments: the first time they kissed, the first time they made love, and the one and only time they'd managed to spend a whole week together when each had contrived an excuse to be away 'on business'. He remembered the hotel room they'd always booked not far from town, which overlooked a walled garden where, having repeatedly made love in their luxurious room, they walked hand in hand in silence, neither daring to voice unbidden thoughts of guilt for fear of breaking the spell.

As similar memories floated into consciousness, his eyes began to lose focus, his gaze became a blur, surroundings receded, sounds faded and he momentarily dozed off until his head fell forward and woke him with a jolt. Passers-by paid no attention but he felt slightly embarrassed as he rubbed his eyes to refocus on his surroundings. And there she was again. On a seat on the opposite side of the pond she sat impassively staring in his direction. Startled, his mind spun out of control. Confusion overwhelmed him. A couple with a small child strolled by, briefly obscuring his view, and when they had passed Yasmin had gone. This proved he must be hallucinating. She couldn't be there one moment and gone the next. It wasn't possible. And if he was hallucinating, then maybe he needed to see a doctor. At the very least, he needed to go home and rest, to properly sleep off the previous evening and rid himself of whatever disturbances were plaguing his mind. The sudden revving of a powerful engine outside the park shattered the tranquillity and so determined him to leave.

Arriving at the park gate, the road was deserted. Still feeling in need of sleep to escape the images that had been haunting him, Mark stepped uncertainly off the pavement just as the revving engine roared and the young driver of the souped-up machine sped around a bend, unaware, unprepared, unconcerned. There was no chance of escape: Mark too slow, the car too fast. Realising the danger, he focused on the opposite pavement and tried to run. And there she stood, watching impassively as Mark was thrown into the air.

But he never hit the ground. Killed instantly by the impact, he continued crossing the road, moving steadily towards Yasmin who now appeared ever more real. In dazed confusion, he kept moving towards her until she reached out and touched him. She was as real as he could remember.

"I've been waiting for you," she greeted.

Mark couldn't answer. Nothing made sense. Had he finally descended into complete, irreversible madness? Despite everything he felt for her, he pulled away. She didn't try to stop him.

"It's all right," she said, calmly.

Mark found his voice. "No, it isn't. I'm dreaming. You're not real."

"I am real, Mark," she said. "Look behind you."

He looked back and saw his body lying in the road, blood everywhere, the car skewed onto the pavement as the young driver sat frantically cursing the damage. But the whole scene was misty and the cursing was faint and muffled as if he were seeing it from another dimension. He looked down at himself, unscathed and just as he had been all morning. Reality dawned.

"But why are you here?" he asked.

For a fleeting moment he saw her change. She was mutilated, a look of horror frozen on her face, her hair matted with blood, her eyes lifeless. Then once again she was as beautiful as he had always remembered.

"That's what he did to me after we moved," she said, seeing that Mark had registered the telepathic image she had just projected to him. "He found out about us and took his revenge. I've been waiting for you ever since. I knew that today was your last day on earth. So I've been watching you, in the library and from the seat across the pond, as I came to meet you."

MISTAKEN IDENTITY

Surely all those parents can't have been wrong? Was it mass hallucination, or what? They'd all read the same announcement in a new free local newspaper they'd found lodged in their letterboxes earlier that week: Santa Claus in his Fairy Grotto ~ All Children Welcome.

All the parents saw it ~ a special children's excursion available at a very reasonable price. It was billed as the perfect opportunity to take a day off from the kids to do some private Christmas shopping. All the details were there and dozens of parents seized the opportunity to drop off their little darlings at the appointed place where assistants dressed as elves entertained them and marshalled them into a hall to sing songs before the excursion. The hall was the only building to have survived the blaze that not long before had annihilated the St Nicholas Community Centre next door and when the families arrived, the smell of burnt out buildings still hung faintly in the air on the derelict site. But the kids were all so excited that they took little notice of their surroundings or even of their mums and dads as they casually waved them goodbye.

At the end of the day the parents returned but none could quite locate the place of departure. All they found was the blackened site alongside the hall, which was now barred and locked. With increasing agitation they searched frantically for the absent elves as puzzlement turned to accusations, but no one they asked seemed to know anything about an excursion and no local residents remembered seeing any children delivered there that morning. Panic mounted amid the lingering smell of charred remains where now only a single resourceful entrepreneur had established temporary premises to sell cooked meats and hamburgers, called Old Nick's. The owner was soon besieged by frenzied parents asking after their children but the old man knew nothing. When they told him they'd seen the advertisement in the new free local newspaper, he pointed to a pile of that publication on the corner of his counter. Several parents grabbed copies to prove their point but they could find no mention of any excursion. All they saw was the announcement they'd seen earlier that week: Satan Claws in His Fiery Ghetto ~ All Children Welcomed.

THE GREY DANCER IN THE TWILIGHT

"No, sir, I wouldn't go into the forest at dusk for any price. There are some things best left alone, undisturbed ~ secrets that belong only to Nature and the Savage Gods. Those who ignore the warnings never return and, believe me, there have been many over the years ~ no trace ever found."

I remember these words well. They came from an old forester I met during one of my evening strolls at the Summer Solstice. The light was just beginning to fade and I remember the look of fear on his weathered face. He had spent his life in the forest and the legends and superstitions associated with it were as certain to him as the sun that rose each morning. I was surprised at meeting him. I'd wandered in that forest many times before and never met a soul. Then there he was, standing motionless in front of me. Deep in thought, I'd almost walked straight into him and was startled by his sudden appearance. After apologising and reorientating myself, we fell into conversation, and anxious not to seem unfriendly, I told him of my lifelong love of the forest and how I often ventured there seeking peace and tranquillity to escape an aggressive and fractured world. I spoke, too, of that particular enchantment when the light changes perceptibly at the hours of dawn or dusk. He listened in silence as I enthused about those magical moments of dawn when creeping light spills across the forest floor, penetrating the foliage and rekindling from slumber the myriad forms of life. But when I spoke of dusk, even as dusk was then approaching, he became perceptibly uneasy as if he had witnessed something of which he dared not speak.

Convinced that one so identified with nature would have some fascinating stories to tell, I pressed him to say something of his experiences. Like myself, he had grown up close to the forest and had sought and welcomed its tranquillity since childhood. He spoke of many enchanting encounters with animals which, growing accustomed to his familiar and unthreatening presence, were emboldened to approach him, allowing him to regard them almost as pets. He knew the hiding places of every species, where to find them, when to leave them alone, and all the phases of their evolution. He told me of a wounded fox he'd once found, how he'd nursed it back to health and how, thereafter, it always came to greet him. He was certain that on one occasion it had saved him from danger by delaying him long enough to avoid a falling tree.

Not entirely convinced, I listened but said nothing to undermine his belief, and taking account of his openness to such a possibility, I ventured on the subject of myths and wondered, perhaps a little too rashly, whether in all his years he had experience of other more elusive creatures. I had in mind those usually found among the pages of legend and folklore, and consistently depicted in paintings of almost every culture over the centuries, such fleeting and magical figures as fauns, centaurs, satyrs, nymphs and unicorns, or perhaps even Pan himself. I wasn't explicit but he understood my meaning instantly and eyed me with suspicion. When I then conjectured that those magical times of changing light seemed to me most felicitous in conjuring such unexpected visions, he stepped away and, raising his voice, as much in fear as indignation, he made that pronouncement which I've never forgotten.

With the first signs of dusk now evident, he turned and walked hastily away as he repeated the words: "Those who ignore the warnings never return," and vanished as unexpectedly as he had first appeared.

It was usually at dusk that the sense of enchantment was most mysterious, especially so on moonless nights, when without the lunar light there was, it seemed, a certain 'glow' that emanated from everything around me. At first, I presumed this was simply the effect of my eyes growing accustomed to the darkness, but there were moments when my vision seemed even clearer than in normal daylight. And on one such occasion, what I saw astounded me.

It was one damp autumn evening. I'd wandered down to the woods in a state of contemplation to ponder in solitude some question or other that had been preoccupying me. The light was fading and a dense mist hovered a foot or two above the ground. Then suddenly I was aware of someone else, an almost translucent figure some distance away that seemed to rise up out of the mist into a clearing where, with arms outstretched and an almost elfin-like agility, it began silently to move as if performing some strange ritual dance before vanishing into the twilight. The scene lasted little more than a minute but was etched in my memory ever afterwards. During those brief moments, time was suspended and when the figure vanished, I was left peering into the gloom, eager to catch just one more glimpse of whatever it was that had so captivated my attention.

My eyes straining against the rising mist and encroaching darkness, I was suddenly struck by the silence of the forest, as if every living creature had stilled itself until that mysterious intruder was safely beyond reach. Against that suspension of activity, all I could hear were random drops of water falling from the trees onto a carpet of dead leaves, sounds that emphasised the depth of that haunted silence. After several minutes everything was normal again and reluctantly I turned to go, taking with me an unexplained image that urged me to return. And return I did, frequently. For the ensuing five evenings I went to the forest at the same time, hoping to repeat my experience and gain a clearer perception of what I'd seen. But it was not to be. Not, that is, until I found myself there by chance the following year at the Spring Equinox.

As always, the surge of energy at spring ~ the burgeoning of trees, the intensity of green and the bustling activity of wildlife ~ fills the air with a sense of renewed hope that is irresistible to anyone attuned to nature and nourished by its spell. Drawn back to the forest, my vision of the previous autumn had dimmed a little but was not forgotten and, given the significance of the day, I dared to wonder whether I would once again witness that strange figure in the twilight.

No sooner had I wondered when I was instantly transfixed. In a clearing some several yards from where I stood, lit by the evening light, a shadowy figure emerged from the trees and, just as before, proceeded to dance with an elegance and agility that suggested a distinct purpose, though what that purpose was remained a mystery. On this occasion, I was able to observe for far longer than previously, during which the dancer's movements seemed to me to beckon, to lure, even to seduce. I remained perfectly still, attention fixed, lest the slightest move might cause the scene to evaporate.

I remembered the forester's warning, uttered with such gravity and fear, and yet, nevertheless, I was increasingly tempted to take the risk of moving closer to the apparition that now captivated my senses with increasingly eloquent movements and a choreography that seemed joyous and inviting. Fully expecting the dancer's sudden disappearance, I took a cautious step forward and as I did so, the only change was in colour. The greyness of that figure, silhouetted against the fading evening light, was enhanced with shimmering peacock colours that made this phantasm appear ever more solid and real. Entranced, I risked a second step and as I did so, the colours of the dancer became enriched and more enticing. In the same moment, the sky beyond grew strangely brighter, completely at odds with the hour and the evening light. Despite every graceful movement of the dancer, who now began to retreat, I once again became aware of the depth of silence that lay over the scene, and I realised that my choice was either to follow, or to remain where I stood and break the spell. I had waited so long to see this apparition again, and yet now, with that sombre voice echoing in my mind, I hesitated. 'Those who ignore the warnings never return.'

But not wanting to lose sight of the dancer, I moved impulsively forward ~ an almost involuntary act ~ as the figure continued to retreat. Recklessly throwing caution to the wind, I hastened after it and, as I did so, somewhere in the depth of my awareness, I understood what it was to be entranced. To 'entrance' creates an entrance. And so it was that as I followed, I lost all sense of time and entered another world. The once fading light of evening became a new dawn. Light enlightened me, illuminating mysteries I had pondered all my life. The dancer vanished into brilliance, leaving me stranded in a landscape of light. All perspectives changed and as my senses adjusted, I found myself at the edge of a different forest inhabited by many animals with which I was familiar and others I could never have imagined, all of which seemed tame and unafraid. I glimpsed, also, several of those mythical beings I had seen in paintings and read about in stories that many dismissed as fanciful. And among them I saw people of every culture in mutual harmony, conversing with each other and communing with the richness of life that surrounded them. In the distance, merging into even brighter light, were vistas so sublime they defied all powers of description and appeared eternal, evoking in me a profound sense of peace.

A moment later, I felt a presence at my side and turned to see a young woman of extreme beauty. She greeted me with a knowing smile. Then she pointed in the direction from which I had arrived, where a dark grey tunnel opened before us. She guided me towards the entrance. It was my opportunity to return to the life I had left behind. But as we approached, all I could hear were screams of anger, cries of fear, voices in argument, and the clash of eternal conflict that reminded me of that aggressive and fractured world from which I had so often sought refuge. A single word formed in my mind, perhaps placed there by my guide: Hell.

As we turned back towards the light, I remembered the forester's warning and his fear of the unknown. It saddened me, for the unknown is knowable. Now also knew precisely why 'no one ever returned'. If only I could tell him. Perhaps one day he will overcome his fear.

TARGETS

Exuberant on his stolen moped, Ryan spotted his target, revved the engine and mounted the pavement, scattering screaming pedestrians in all directions. The young woman unable to tear her attention away from her phone, shrieked with outrage and shock as it was snatched from her hand and the rider disappeared, weaving his way dangerously through the traffic. It was the work of an instant.

Back with his gang, Ryan was the hero they all envied as he brandished the trophy for which he already had a buyer in mind. Inspired by his latest feat, two of the gang immediately sped off to do the same, or something even better. Competition was rife as they all tried to out-perform each other.

That afternoon, Ryan ditched the moped, smashing it in the process, and set off to find another. If you knew where to look it was easy to locate some rich kid's pride and joy left unattended and insecure. He'd stolen four in the past three months and never used the same one more than a few times. That way he'd never been identified and never encountered the police.

The police were worse than useless, too afraid to pursue a moped once the rider removed his helmet in case he was injured or killed in the pursuit, resulting in the police being prosecuted. Government cutbacks meant fewer police on the streets, political correctness tied the hands of those few, and Ryan's gang became the scourge of the city, modern-day highwaymen in all but name.

With police resources stretched to breaking point and disillusioned officers leaving in droves, Government targets played straight into the hands of the gang who made rich pickings from anyone they had in their sights. Easy targets were tourists, inattentive and unfamiliar with their surroundings, and of course, the legion of addicted young men and women unable to tear their gaze from their phones in the street.

But phones were relatively easy to grab and as competition in the gang intensified, some returned with briefcases, laptops, handbags and even designer watches, anything that challenged the skills of the rider. These blatant thefts regularly hit the headlines, another source of pride for Ryan and his gang. They laughed at the ease with which they could snatch a bag when the target walked too close to the edge of the pavement, unaware of any danger.

The police, still at a loss, had other things to focus on, not least the threat of bombers who despised the way of life led in the country that had given them refuge. They were the enemy within, a higher priority than tearaways on mopeds who knew this only too well. With common sense and basic caution they could get away with anything. Not one of Ryan's gang had ever been interviewed by the police about moped theft or anything else.

They congregated in parks or back streets, always changing their rendezvous to avoid attention. At the end of every day they met in high spirits to share their stories, to show off their spoils, and to gloat at their stupid victims and the pathetic police. They celebrated the latest headlines, criticising authorities and urging increased public awareness. The same edition reported the latest bomb threat that was consuming all police resources, useful information for the gang, making them feel invincible as they mocked and jeered, determined to take advantage of this distraction. The following day was a field day as every member of the twelve-strong gang turned out to cause mayhem on the streets and boast about their exploits.

Meanwhile, all police attention was focused on a suspect who had been under surveillance for weeks. This was the day they made their move. Tracking him on street cameras, they seized and arrested their target. During interviews, the suspect repeatedly protested his innocence. The backpack he'd been wearing yielded nothing suspicious. But where was the bag he'd been carrying in his hand? Just as the question was asked, a blinding explosion elsewhere in the city sent commuters rushing for cover as they passed by the central park where a group of youths had just gathered.

A dozen named victims of the tragedy were listed and mourned next day in the evening press, all young men with, as the report put it, 'their whole lives still ahead of them'. But for once, there were no reported incidents of street theft.

A CERTAIN MAGIC

I killed a child today. He was the first, but there will be more. I couldn't help it. Some ancient instinct arose deep within me and made me do it. Now I am exiled. Cut off from the rest of humanity. Hated. Anathema. In the eyes of others I am beyond redemption. I hide in the forest. I hear them searching for me but I am not afraid. Have I not as much right to live as they? They who go to war and think nothing of killing anyone they deem to be the enemy. They kill entire families, including children. They have a choice. I have none.

I was destined to kill. It is the way of nature. Look around. Every species preys on another. Is that God's great plan? They ~ not I ~ speak of God, especially when they kill those they regard as 'the enemy'. Every creature is true to its own nature. I am true to mine. I kill to live. They kill for principle or pleasure.

I come from an ancient family, not confined to one continent but spread across the world. We exist alongside the rest of humanity, undetected, unremarkable, until one day a son is born. The seventh son of a seventh son. There is a superstition about such boys. We prefer not to believe it. But nature will do what nature does. And one day, when that boy becomes a man, that ancient instinct from an alien past is reignited. I was born a boy. I became a man. And then I became a wolf. The superstition is true. It is the magic of lycanthropy. I have no control over the creature within. Only a silver bullet can destroy me.

Now the moon is full and I can hear the hunters coming closer but I am not afraid. I have superhuman strength ~ and I am hungry. They do not believe in superstition ~ except for their God, in whose name they kill ~ and so I know they will have no silver bullets.

THE YANUTHIM

by Richard Howard

Surprise, fear and awe possessed every inhabitant of the rural community when they awoke one morning to find a gigantic ovoid occupying the middle of the village green. As big as the local Manor House, it was shiny, metallic and perfectly smooth with no trace of seams or rivets to hold it together, a highly polished egg from which the morning sun was reflected with an uncanny beauty. Curious and baffled, people cautiously gathered around, but of those who approached closer, none quite dared reach out to touch it.

Within two hours, word had spread to the wider community and the rumble of military vehicles filled the country lanes. Inhabitants were forcibly evacuated to a remote compound where they were sworn to silence and made to sign an official secrets document before being released while the village was cordoned off.

From all around the world, identical ovoids were being reported as governments closed ranks, taking strict measures against anyone who had witnessed the phenomenon. Desperate to remain in control, it was crucial not to admit they had no knowledge of these structures or how to approach them. But none of this mattered. By the end of the day the eggs had 'hatched', releasing a gas that would poison every living creature on the planet.

The Yanuthim were an advanced civilisation inhabiting a planet many thousands of light years from these events. Technology enabled them to travel vast distances in a micro-fraction of the time that had once been necessary. Scientific knowledge of hyper-sonic telescopes, developed by their finest minds over hundreds of generations, enabled them to identify potentially inhabitable planets in other galaxies where they could establish new colonies to ensure their continued survival and evolution. This became increasingly necessary as they quickly drained all planetary energy and natural resources wherever they went.

Constantly scanning the skies, emitting signals to locate signs of life elsewhere, there was always wry amusement when an occasional weak response, indicated a scientific community woefully inferior to their own. There was nothing to suggest they were anything less than supreme masters of all they surveyed throughout every known galaxy and universe as they continued to seek new planets to colonise.

Once a hospitable location had been confirmed, the first requirement was to cleanse it of all existing life forms that might be hostile to new inhabitants. For this specific purpose they had developed the ovoids that were targeted to land at strategic points all over the chosen planet, ensuring no unforeseen opposition when their landing craft began to arrive. A temporal side effect of this advanced technology erased all trace of the planet's inhabitants throughout its history.

Ultra-sensitive technology allowed them to monitor the cleansing process in considerable detail. They watched impatiently as signs of life slowed to nothing all over the chosen planet. Corpses of every species littered the ground as they began to decay, accelerated by a component in the lethal gas to leave an uncluttered, fertile landscape for the Yanuthim. Birds fell from the sky in mid-flight, plummeting to the ground, disintegrating in seconds, to leave an eerie silence broken only by sounds of dissolving, liquifying flesh. The whole process was achieved within a single rotation of the planet as the Yanuthim prepared their vast flotilla of super-craft for migration.

Over millennia, the Yanuthim occupied any planet they discovered where life could be sustained with maximum individual freedom and minimum need for survival-technology.

While the atmospheres of some planets required the use of inconvenient apparatus for basic survival ~ which could always be configured with their advanced technology ~ others allowed complete freedom to breathe and move about freely. Survival by whatever means across vast distances and aeons of time was one of the great strengths of the Yanuthim. Any other race they encountered faced insurmountable opposition.

Several other highly advanced species with lesser technology on other planets observed the Yanuthim migrations, which showed up on their monitors with alarming frequency. As they scanned deep space, tracking signs of migrating forces, many ceased transmitting signals in order not to attract the attention of such an all-powerful alien force. But then something completely inexplicable happened.

The Yanuthim had identified their next planet for occupation and ovoids were launched to commence the cleansing process. As they landed all over the terrain, signs of increased activity among the life-forms living there were monitored from light years away. It was a familiar pattern. First a flurry of activity, then as the gas was released, nothing. Time to commence migration.

To the other intelligences observing this process, not only did all signs of activity on the target planet cease, but the Yanuthim themselves vanished without trace. It was scientifically untenable. For countless days and nights, different species on different planets searched deep into space for any sign of the feared Yanuthim. Finding no trace of them, they became cautiously optimistic. Baffled by what they had witnessed, a thousand possible unconvincing explanations were advanced, none of which came close the truth.

It was a one-in-a-quadrillion chance but it happened, nevertheless. The last planet targeted by the Yanuthim was the one on which their own race had originated aeons before, and because their method of cleansing eradicated all trace of the occupants' history, they exterminated themselves and ceased to exist. In a parallel universe, life on all the planets they had colonised carried on as if nothing had happened.

E*L*E*A*N*O*R

A Love Story

Even from a distance, her beauty took my breath away. The first time I saw her was late one balmy summer evening as I sat watching dragonflies skimming the lake, darting from one waterlily to the next, hovering motionless in mid-air with wings moving so fast they were almost invisible, like apparitions from another world. It was at that very moment that she caught my eye, as though her dress was woven from the very same gossamer threads that kept the dragonflies aloft. As the sun sank and the air cooled, bats appeared, swooping silently from the azure dusk where once the dragonflies had been, adding an air of mystery to that vision of pure beauty that had captured my attention from the far side of the lake. Her movements were of such slender grace, her dark shoulder-length hair flowing against her pale dress as she paced back and forth, as if in contemplation, before she finally stepped towards an arched doorway set in an ancient, weather-beaten wall and disappeared beyond it. The door closed without the slightest sound, which further piqued my curiosity and compelled me to rise from my seat and walk the circumference of the lake before the last vestiges of light had completely faded.

Arriving at the wall in a luminous half-light, I couldn't immediately find any door at all, although in the irregular brickwork at one point there did appear the outline of an arch-shaped pattern that might once have been a door, long ago sealed up. Surely, I thought, this cannot have been the lady's means of entry; there must be a real door somewhere. As the sun was finally extinguished, it was replaced by the faintest trace of moonlight, allowing me to satisfy my curiosity and explore a little further. Feeling my way along the weathered bricks that still emitted heat from the day, my search was eventually rewarded as I alighted on the only door I could find. It was made of heavy, splintered wood upon which an iron ring served as the only handle. I grasped it firmly, anticipating the need for a strong hand, but it would not move. How, I wondered, did so slight a girl open it with such ease when it would not budge an inch for me? And then I realised it must have been locked from within, which, being the case and the lady in question in possession of a key, must surely suggest that she was the owner or the keeper of whatever lay beyond.

Dragonfly dreams haunted my restless sleep for the ensuing nights when it was impossible to dispel from my mind the seductive image from across the lake. By day and night my thoughts repeatedly returned to her, as though she had usurped my life altogether and become the new sun in my universe, which now revolved solely around her fragrant light, caught in a whirlpool that drew me ever closer to its centre, luring me back time and again to the memory of that fateful evening and beckoning me to return. While I knew I had no choice but to return, I wondered how one mere mortal could exert such influence and power over another from such a distance. I wondered, too, whether she knew that she had captured my heart and was patiently waiting for me. Or perhaps she was oblivious of anyone who fell under her spell and I, like an insignificant comet, would pass by unobserved in her richly-jewelled universe of fantastic landscapes and exotic dreams. Now, more than anything, it was imperative that I find out.

I hadn't long moved to the vicinity and was still becoming acquainted with the local area. The extensive parkland that had been the setting for my alluring vision had much within it that was yet to be explored. It was all new and unknown to me and I wasn't entirely sure that I even had right of access because it was unclear whether this was, in fact, a public park or private property. In the absence of any notice to clarify the situation, I had simply taken advantage and was ready to make my apologies in the event of being challenged. The fact that I saw no one else there might have suggested that I was, indeed, trespassing but there could have been other reasons that I found myself alone that day and it seemed to augur well that on my first visit I should have been so enchanted. There was, I thought, something fateful about this event.

It was more than a week before I had the opportunity to return. Returning anywhere to try to re-live a treasured experience is usually a mistake and I knew this before I set out and therefore, eager as I was, I tried to keep my hopes and expectations to a reasonable proportion. But however much I told myself that I might never again see that wondrous vision of perfect beauty, I hoped to with all my heart. And my heart, like it or not, was now, it seemed, inextricably entwined with hers. She might not know it, but in my passion, I prayed that she could feel it, because the prospect of an unrequited love was far too painful to contemplate.

As I arrived at the lake, the afternoon sun drew from every flower a radiant glow as if responding to the warmth of its touch. Purple, yellow, pink and green flooded my senses as the water glistened and a heady perfume from the Himalayan Balsam evoked in me dreams more passionate and dangerous than I could ever have created from my own imagination. It is true that with passion comes danger, which is the risk we take when we heed the will of the heart. We create a web of dreams filled with idealised hopes and desires towards which we blindly strive until, for those less fortunate, they realise they are helplessly trapped in that web of their own making. From within my reverie, I was determined to avoid such a fate.

Sitting in the shade of a tree that sheltered me from the heat of the sun, I gazed across the lake and tried to conjure the image that I longed to see again. Half-closing my eyes, I allowed them to shift perspective and constantly refocus in every possible endeavour to summon her into being. Using all my willpower, I tried to see beyond the mundane and penetrate the mystery of that ancient wall, beyond which I believed the object of my love to exist. I projected my longing heart with its passionate message to soar above the wall and to find her, wherever she was, so that she would know that I was waiting for her and so reveal herself. Such were my endeavours but all to no avail.

I sat entranced, lost in my dreams, fending off the sense of desolation that hammered on my heart, but I would not be so easily defeated. As my impatient longing gave way to an insistent ache, I began to reason with myself. Why should she respond to my summons? True love does not make such demands but waits and endures with gentle patience. That must be the way to demonstrate my love. And so, with no incentive to leave, I remained seated, once again marvelling at the dragonflies and dozing fitfully until the sun began to fade. Then suddenly wide awake and with a sense of déjà vu, I realised that the hour must have come when I first beheld she for whom I now waited. And there she was in all her grace and elegance, pacing back and forth, just as before.

Seized with excitement, instantly I ran towards the lake, tracing a path along its perimeter, unable to tear my eyes from the object of my dreams. Then, a moment later I deliberately slowed my pace, suddenly afraid that I might startle her, and proceeded to walk, mesmerised by the elegance of her every movement. But as I drew near, just as in a dream, my footsteps grew increasingly leaden and sluggish while, at the same moment, she began to walk towards the door. Desperately fighting against the heaviness of my body, I cried out for her to stop but, once again, I was thwarted and, despairing, I watched as she passed beyond the door that closed silently behind her. A moment later, my legs were alive again and I ran to the door but, just as before, it was locked.

Heavy-hearted and alone once more with my thoughts, in the ensuing days, the sight of her vanishing beyond that door played out repeatedly in my mind. I had come so close and with every step had seen her beauty magnified to a radiance beyond imagining. And the closer I came, the more I wanted her. I saw her crimson lips and imagined her kisses, as sweet as honey and roses. I could feel the caress of her soft hand on my cheek. I could hear the delicate cadence of her voice as she returned my love and whispered the words I longed to hear. But now I knew exactly the time and place where I might see her again. I would abandon my seat across the lake and wait beside the door, ready to declare my love. The opportunity could not come soon enough.

But fate continued to torment me. A day later I succumbed to a severe fever that consumed me for almost a week. As the burning raged within me, so in equal measure did my frustrated desire, and when it had finally run its course, I was so exhausted that I could barely bestir myself and remained in dire need of several more days to regain my full strength. All this time, drifting in and out of delirium, my pain was multiplied a thousandfold as I remembered the closing door that shut me out from my heart's desire. The more I was thwarted ~ as if the amorous gods were toying with my feelings and taking a perverse pleasure in my suffering ~ the more desperate I became to finally confront the love of my life who I now began to fear would think I had so casually abandoned her. Eventually the day arrived when I felt able to leave my room and so, fired up and determined, I set out to meet my destiny.

I arrived at the lake before sunset on yet another idyllic summer evening, again unaware of anyone else in the vicinity. It was as if this enchanted place had been reserved especially for me alone ~ that is to say, myself, the dragonflies and, as I often thought of her now, my dragonfly princess. While the sun was still sinking, I resumed the seat I had frequented on my previous visits and sat gazing at the stillness of the lake, above which several darting swallows were diving to catch insects and where the water skaters miraculously strode across the unbroken surface.

Then, as the light began to wane, the moment came for me to take up my position beside the door. With some trepidation but a determined step, I walked the short distance to the ancient wall with which I had become so familiar. But as I approached in the rapidly increasing gloom, imagine my surprise to find the door unlocked and slightly ajar. Slowly and cautiously, I moved closer, in awe of what I might find, but before I could step within, she appeared. She was smiling such a smile as I had never seen before, encompassing all the warmth of a thousand summers, mingled with recognition, delight and welcome. As my ecstatic heart pounded, I was speechless and hoped upon hope that the smile I returned would convey all the subtleties and complexities of the deep love that she inspired in me. For several moments we stood, our eyes locked, until eventually, turning away, she raised one hand and beckoned me to follow.

As the door closed silently behind us, night had finally fallen and I shivered as a sudden chill embraced my whole body. As far as the eye could see, a cemetery stretched out before me ~ and beyond that wall it was winter. Despite the flimsiness of her pale gown, my dragonfly princess appeared unaffected by the cold as she slowly began to walk on ahead, turning occasionally with a smile that seemed to convey all the love I craved and beckoning for me to follow. Silently we traced many a long pathway, winding between row upon row of moonlit graves, thick with frost, the tombs of the forgotten and the long-dead. Shivering, I glanced up and saw only stars and the silver moon that touched her flowing hair as she led me deeper into the cemetery until we reached the very centre, which was our destination. Here we stopped and she pointed towards an imposing mausoleum above the door of which was elaborately engraved a single word:

E*L*E*A*N*O*R

Elsewhere on the façade I read the inscription:

Our beloved daughter, taken from us by the fever long before her time: 1843 ~ 1860.

I looked at her as she continued to point towards the mausoleum, where now the door swung wide open. Standing in the moonlight, she seemed so lost. I longed to comfort her but was transfixed by her beauty and did not move. Then her smile grew wistful and a distant, faraway look descended on her countenance as if suddenly I appeared to her as no more than a ghost from another land and, turning away, she began to ascend the steps to her tomb. My heart in turmoil, I ran towards her as she approached the open door, glancing back at me with such hope and longing. For a moment, I hesitated but I knew that if I did not follow, I would lose her forever. And so I stepped inside the tomb. As the door closed firmly behind us, never again to be opened, the only source of light was her radiance. Now at last we are together.

* * *

"What an extraordinary communication," said the Colonel.

"Yes, I've never known anything so long and detailed from the other side," said the medium. "I thought you'd be interested," she added.

"Over how many séances did you receive this message?"

"It was conveyed during several sessions in the course of the past few months."

"But I wonder why?" the Colonel mused.

"Well, that puzzled me, too, but then I read that the old cemetery on the other side of town has recently been deconsecrated and sold to developers. It's been locked and inaccessible for decades but I think that might have been what prompted this poignant communication. Of course, it's scandalous that here we are in 2089, and there's not the slightest respect for past traditions. Bit by bit they've been tearing down tombstones, ploughing up the ground, and even the mausoleum is in the process of being demolished. And that's what makes this so interesting."

"How exactly?"

"Well, according to a report in the local news, when they opened the mausoleum, they discovered inside not one, but two skeletons. This was a monument built by a wealthy, grieving family for their young daughter, a girl of only 17. It wasn't a family tomb. It was designed solely to commemorate her.

"As for the communication, I think he just needed to tell his story before all trace of his beloved Eleanor is erased. We know that those who have moved on can still be aware of events happening in this world, especially when those events have been so emotionally charged. Plainly, he was a passionate and determined man and it was important for him that the true facts be known. Others might not be able to explain the presence of a second skeleton, but I think you and I now know differently. Wouldn't you say so?"

TREACHERY

There are many forms of treason, treachery and betrayal ~ some political, some domestic, some intensely personal. I see from today's newspaper that a man in his late eighties has been murdered in what police believe to be an apparently motiveless crime. He was bludgeoned to death and left in the open to be found. There was no attempt to hide the body, implying either carelessness or arrogance. Or perhaps whoever it was wants to be discovered. Some people are like that. They want the publicity, the notoriety, to be feared. I wonder why? Could it be because they feel so insignificant or inadequate that this is the only way to become noticed? People are a mystery.

I once used to fantasise about killing my father. He was a bully at home but charming to strangers ~ a real Jekyll and Hyde. You never really know what lurks behind the mask of sociability. I suppose we are all a potential Jesus Christ or Adolf Hitler. Everything depends upon circumstances and the pressures we experience.

Yes, I fantasised about killing him but, as life went on and he mellowed in old age, I was able to forgive. Forgiving is good but one should never forget, otherwise what have we learned? Perhaps fantasies function in that way ~ they allow us to go through the motions, conjure the images and gain some sense of satisfaction without actually doing the deed and running the risk of being caught. I quickly realised that there would be little point in killing him, only to languish in prison for the rest of my life. What would that have achieved? No, one has to let these things go and move on. Everyone has their trials to face in life and he was mine. The humiliation of his jokes at my expense, the routine undermining and belittling, the constant criticism, these were an everyday reality. But I got used to them. Then there were the random acts of violence. That was more difficult. It was the randomness that made everything so fearful because when something like that happens out of the blue for no discernible reason, even if it only occurs infrequently, the threat is ever-present, and so you live in constant fear that it could happen at any moment. I imagine lots of kids go through such things and find their own way to deal with them. I did.

Of course, the perfect murder would be one where the murderer had no traceable connection to the victim. Something gratuitous, random and unexplained. That would really fox the police. A savage act committed simply because the opportunity was there and perhaps the perpetrator was curious to know what it felt like to have that sense of power ~ the power of life or death. I suppose you'd need to be a very damaged person to want to play God in that way. It's hard to comprehend.

Now here we are three months later and the papers report that the police are as mystified as ever, having made no progress in the absence of any motive. That's the beauty of a random killing. It's the motive and the connection to the killer that usually provide the most useful clues.

Of course, I knew they'd never find me because I'd never met the man before. I only found out who he was by reading the papers. Turns out he was of east European extraction and suspected of being a concentration camp guard but there was never enough evidence to charge him. Oh well, I suppose what goes around, comes around. As soon as I saw him, he reminded me of my father. The light was fading fast, as it often does on these beautiful autumn evenings, and there was no one about. Providence provided me with a fallen branch lying on the grass verge only a few feet from where I was walking. It was a spontaneous impulse. I picked it up and clubbed him from behind. I'd left the scene almost before he hit the ground and saw no one from that moment until I was back indoors pouring myself a drink. All I have to do is sit it out and stay silent. To be perfectly honest, I'm slightly shocked by what I did. Maybe Jekyll and Hyde can be passed on through the genes. He did look uncannily like my father. I suppose that's what triggered my response, which is quite understandable. I feel relatively safe from the police because there's nothing to connect me with him.

The only thing that troubles me is that he has followed me here and I can see him now, sitting in my armchair with an accusing look. I feel I want to kill him but that's impossible because I already have. At least, I think it's the man I met outside, or is it my father? They look so alike, it's hard to tell. Whoever it is, he's been here now all this time and has no intention of leaving. He's taken up residence and I can tell from his expression that it's his intention to drive me mad. But I won't let that happen.

Wait! Who was that who just passed my window? I could have sworn it was my father. Oh well, I'll catch him next time. Meanwhile, I suppose I must endure that baleful gaze of whoever it is who mocks me from my armchair. But I'm sure I can learn to forgive him, just as I did my father.

APPEARANCES

She woke from a deep sleep, glanced at the clock, threw back the covers and hastened to the bathroom. The flat was cold. It was three in the morning and the central heating hadn't come on yet. Having relieved herself, she pulled her nightdress tightly around her and made a bee line for her warm bed. What it was that diverted her attention, she didn't know but, despite the intense cold, she stopped briefly to peep out between the curtains. Just as she suspected, a thin layer of snow covered the ground, glowing eerily beneath the street lights. What she didn't expect was the figure standing motionless in the pool of light shed by the lamp directly opposite her second floor flat. The man wore a broad-brimmed hat and an overcoat but no one in their right mind, she thought, would be standing there at that hour in the freezing cold without some dubious motive. And what worried her more was that he was staring directly up at her window.

She hesitated a moment longer but from such a distance and the angle of light, she couldn't see the man's face. Shivering, she darted back to the warmth of her bed. As she huddled beneath the covers, she wished she hadn't stopped to look out. If only she'd gone straight back to bed she would probably have drifted easily into sleep but now she couldn't erase from her mind the image she had just seen. Perhaps he was only looking up at her window because he saw the curtains move. But why was he there at all?

When she woke again it was daylight and she reached out to silence the alarm ten minutes before it was due to go off. Despite the thick curtains, she could tell it was an intensely bright day as she got up and began the ritual of preparing to leave in time for the train to work.

The winter sunlight reflecting off the thin covering of snow was blinding as she stepped outside to join other familiar faces heading for the station at the bottom of the road. She appreciated living close to the railway because it allowed her those extra precious minutes every morning. Locking the front door, she glanced across the street and suddenly remembered the figure she'd seen standing there in the middle of the night. Two young schoolboys chased each other around the lamppost before racing off. She was tempted for a moment to cross over and look at the spot where she'd seen the figure but there was no point and, anyway, she needed to head for the station.

At the end of the journey, the train jolted across multiple points with jarring metallic squeaks to arrive at the platform. Dozens of people simultaneously stood up, clinging to overhead straps, trying to keep their balance as they waited for the doors to open. Only then did she vacate her seat to join them. As the crowd moved forward, she caught sight of a figure at the far end of the carriage who reminded her of the man beneath the lamp. He wore a broad-brimmed hat pulled forward, obscuring his face. It gave her a start, but since she hadn't seen his face, she couldn't know it was the same person. It was just a fleeting impression but there was something about the way he was standing that convinced her it was him. The unexpected and unexplained image of the previous night, and especially the fact that he was looking up at her window, seemed to have embedded itself in her consciousness, making her agitated and cautious. She looked again but the crowd was moving and the figure had gone. On the platform she looked everywhere but saw no one resembling the person she had glimpsed in the carriage. Then, jostled by the crowd, she was swept towards the ticket barriers and the sight of a work colleague close by engaged her attention as they fell easily into conversation.

The walk to the office wasn't far and they always took a short cut along a narrow alleyway that led from the station concourse to the part of town where they worked. Other commuters pushed impatiently past them as their steps slowed down in conversation.

"How was your weekend?" asked her friend. "Did you see that bloke you were telling me about?"

"No, he didn't turn up. We were supposed to meet at the cinema. I only waited ten minutes. He didn't text and I'm not going to hang around for anyone who's late. Plenty more fish in the sea. What about you?"

"Yeah, we got it together. It was better than last time. He came to my place, we fucked, then he took me out for dinner, back to mine, fucked again, slept like a dog and when I woke up he'd gone."

"What, no note or anything?"

"No, but that's OK. It quite suited me really. I needed some space. He'll be back when he's ready. He always is."

She was very fond of this friend, liked her openness and no-nonsense attitudes, and was grateful that she'd been approached by her as soon as she started at the company. It was precisely because of her openness that they had straight become confidantes. Throughout the morning's work, the image of the figure looking up at her window intruded repeatedly into her thoughts, so when lunchtime came and they met as usual in the restroom, she decided to tell her friend. When the conversation lulled and the opportunity arose, she hesitated.

"You all right?" the friend asked.

"Yes… no… I don't know. There was this bloke…"

Her friend's eyes lit up. "Yes," she urged.

"It was the middle of the night and he was standing under the street light opposite my flat in the freezing cold."

"So? Some nutter."

"Maybe. But he was looking up at my window."

"Nutters do things like that. Trust me. Was he doing anything else?"

"No. Just standing there looking up at the window."

"Did you recognise him?"

"I couldn't see his face. It was in shadow. He was wearing some kind of hat and he was too far away to see clearly. Anyway I was half asleep. I only got up for a pee but something made me look out before going back to bed. It was scary."

"You sure it wasn't a dream?"

"I've been thinking about it ever since and I'm sure he was really there."

"You haven't been seeing any weirdos you haven't told me about, have you?"

"No."

"What about that bloke who wanted you to dress up in some kind of uniform and boss him about?"

"No, that was over a year ago and, anyway, I've seen him around with another woman. He always avoids looking at me if I see him in the street."

"You never know with weirdos."

"No, if it was him, it wouldn't bother me. But there was something about this bloke last night that was a bit sinister."

"It's probably nothing. Maybe he was waiting for someone else and saw you looking out."

"Maybe but it seems unlikely he'd be waiting for someone when it's snowing at three in the morning."

"It wasn't the guy who stood you up, was it? Did he leave flowers on your doorstep?"

"No," she said emphatically, with a tentative half-smile at her friend's attempts to make light of it. "Honestly, it freaked me. I can't stop thinking about it."

"What about that little bloke in the warehouse who can't take his eyes off you?"

"It definitely wasn't him. Anyway, he wouldn't. No, this bloke was much bigger."

"Well, I guess all you can do is see if he's there again tonight."

That night she went to bed late and slept undisturbed until the alarm woke her. Reassured by the daylight and out of sheer curiosity, she went straight to the window. He was there, looking directly up at her, just as before. She'd been certain he wouldn't be, and seeing him in the daylight shocked her. He wore a long overcoat, tailored in a style she hadn't seen before, and a wide-brimmed hat bearing no resemblance to any current fashion, tilted forward and obscuring his face. As soon as she saw him, he looked away and walked leisurely towards the station.

She wasn't sure which disturbed her more: the fact that he was there covertly in the middle of the night, or that he should brazenly show himself in daylight. The thought of going to the station herself within the next half hour preyed on her mind as she ate breakfast. But if he had gone there already, he'd surely have caught a train long before she arrived to catch hers.

Walking to the station she made a point of noticing everyone around her. They were mostly the usual faces and she saw no one wearing a hat and a long overcoat. The train journey passed routinely, passengers ignoring each other, plugged into electronic devices, deaf to the world in headphones, looking vacantly into space or gazing fixedly at screens. She had ample opportunity to scrutinise them all without seeming intrusive and was relieved not to see the man in question. The doors hissed and closed and the train pulled away from the penultimate stop. And that was when she saw him. Not on the train but through the window. There he was just a few feet away on the other side of the glass, standing alone on the platform, looking straight at her as the train accelerated out of the station.

Her heart pounded as she tried to see his face, but he was out of sight before she could fully turn around. For a fleeting instant they had looked directly at each other and she was certain he was watching her. Aware of her sudden movement, a woman sitting opposite glanced up, looking concerned. Their eyes briefly met and she managed a weak smile to convey that she was OK. But she wasn't. The man through the window wore the same broad-brimmed hat and although, however fleetingly, they had looked directly at each other, she had no memory of a single facial feature. Either his face was obscured by shadow or he didn't have a face.

Her friend at work had called in sick, so her day at the office was punctuated only by lightweight conversation with a few of the other women and at lunchtime she sat alone in the restroom, barely able to concentrate on a magazine. Most of the employees were women but there were a few young lads who worked the warehouse and whose presence, if they came into the restroom, always had the effect of subduing the general conversation. It was rare that they all came in together because the warehouse couldn't be left unattended but, for whatever reason, today was an exception and suddenly the level of rowdiness increased as they all arrived in high spirits and a couple of them, uninvited, grabbed vacant chairs at tables occupied by of some of the girls. Sitting alone, she failed to look inconspicuous and was suddenly the resentful target of the boy who was always watching her.

"Whatcha reading?" the boy asked.

"What's it look like?" she replied.

"No need to be sarcy. What's yer name?"

"Cleopatra."

"Really? No, you're kidding me!"

"Yes, I'm kidding!"

"So, what's yer name?"

"None of your business."

She was definitely *not* in the mood. She pushed back her chair and began to walk away.

"Oh, get you! What is it? Time of the month?"

Stopping abruptly, she turned around and threw the magazine, hitting him squarely in the face. Instantly he was out of his chair, heading after her but was stopped by one of the others.

"Forget it, mate. She ain't worth it. Stuck up bitch."

That night, she lay in bed thinking about the incident in the restroom. It both frightened and angered her. She felt invaded by unwelcome attentions. It was bad enough worrying about the man she was convinced was watching her, without a little prat like that having a go. Unable to sleep, she got up and made some tea, switched on her computer, wrote some overdue emails, then ordered a couple of sweaters and few other items from one of her favourite online stores. Eventually she grew tired and felt ready for sleep. She knew she shouldn't but it was impossible not to take a quick peep between the curtains. Sure enough, he was there, looking up at her window.

Instantly, her anger reignited. She grabbed her clothes, pulled on her coat and boots and ran downstairs. In her pocket she had a high pitched alarm and an illegal pepper spray, all ready to use. She knew it was dangerous but she didn't care. After the first landing, she raced down the second flight, ran the length of the hallway to the front door and threw it wide open. The lamp opposite glowed brightly on the snowy ground but there was no one there.

Cautiously, all senses primed, she ventured out into the street. She stopped to listen but the only sound that reached her was a muffled, distant train docking in a siding for the night. As the cold penetrated her half-buttoned coat, she peered in every direction, stunned and angry, before turning slowly back towards the front door. Once inside, she climbed the stairs, baffled by the absence of anyone beneath the lamp. Only then did the thought occur to her that maybe he had known what she was going to do and had entered the flats while she was outside, leaving the front door open. In her haste she had also left the door of her own flat unlocked.

The thought terrified her but she had no option but to carry on up the second flight and face whoever might be waiting for her. Reaching the door of her flat, she slowly pushed it open, her hand firmly on the pepper spray. All was quiet and still as she entered, leaving the door ajar in case she needed a hasty retreat. If that happened, she would set off her pocket alarm and wake up the whole block, and any intruder would be confronted by a dozen angry neighbours. One by one, she cautiously checked each room: sitting room, kitchen, bathroom, hallway cupboards, and finally the bedroom. There was no one. Relieved, she quickly returned to the front door and locked it.

It took a while to regain composure as she sat in her coat puzzling over what had happened but she was pleased with herself for having had the guts to go down and face whoever it was. But now she was left with doubts about what was real and what she'd been seeing. She was certain about the man beneath the lamp. Her friend had asked if it was a dream, but she was equally sure she'd seen him in the train one day and on the platform that very morning. Eventually she gave up speculating and undressed for bed. On her way, she checked the window. He was back.

And so he was every night for the rest of the week. She never saw him arrive but whenever she looked out after dark, he was usually there. Once or twice the space beneath the lamp was empty but whenever she looked again, he had returned and, unfailingly, was looking up at her window. Temperatures remained just below zero and, day and night in the early winter weather, tiny flecks of snow hung in the air, ensuring the thin layer underfoot was constantly replenished.

Each day during her train journeys, when she was least expecting it, at some point she was convinced she saw the same figure nearby, either on the far side of a crowd or watching from a point she couldn't reach, even though it was only a short distance away. It was Friday before her friend returned to work and she was able to update her on what had been happening.

"You actually went down in the middle of the night?" the friend exclaimed.

"Yes. I was angry. I just want to know what's going on. Then, as if that wasn't enough, that little squirt from the warehouse was bugging me here in the restroom. We almost came to blows. I'd have smacked him in the face if one of his mates hadn't stopped him coming at me. I'm so fed up with it."

"I know, I've had similar things. But this bloke who's been watching you, all he does is look up at your window? Right?"

"Yes, but it's creepy. He was even there one morning, in broad daylight."

"And he never approaches you?"

"No. He's always at a distance where I can't confront him. Maybe he's waiting for the right moment to do whatever he intends, but I'm buggered if I'm going to let him rule my life. I'm not going to stop doing things because of him."

Suddenly an angry voice joined the conversation.

"Don't think you're going to get away with that, you cow," said the boy from the warehouse.

They both turned to see him standing over their table.

"What d'you want?" the friend challenged.

"Not you. Her," he said jabbing the air with his finger. "She made me look stupid the other day."

"It doesn't take anyone else to make you look stupid, mate," said the friend.

"Shut yer mouth. This is none of your business."

"Well, it's my business when I'm talking to my friend, so piss off and get lost, you pathetic little creep."

"What are you, a couple of lezzos?"

"With blokes like you around, any girl would be. Now, piss off."

Deflated, the boy backed away with his parting shot.

"I'll get you," he said pointing at his intended target.

As soon as he left the restroom, they cracked up laughing.

"What a tosser," said the friend. "Anyway, sorry I wasn't around to chat the last couple of days, only Romeo turned up again and we just couldn't keep our hands off each other."

"I thought you were ill."

"Yeah, love sick. That's an illness, ain't it? Getting serious. Says he wants to come back tomorrow and stay the weekend."

"Good for you," she said. She was so grateful to be able to share things and feel less alone.

On Saturday, she got up late and caught a train to look around the shops. She'd checked the window before going to bed the night before and, sure enough, the same figure was standing beneath the lamp. On the journey into town she kept a look out but didn't see him. Alighting from the train, she took the usual route along the alleyway into the part of town where the best shops were. She fancied treating herself to a new winter coat and knew exactly where to begin looking. A moment later she heard several voices and muffled laughter approaching from behind. Then someone shouted at her. She recognised the voice of the boy from the warehouse. There was no one else in the alleyway. Unable to turn back and with some distance to go before reaching the street at the far end, she instinctively quickened her step. She knew she could never outrun them but if she kept up the pace, she hoped they might leave her alone. Then the shouting became more threatening and they started running. At the same moment, a figure in a long dark coat and broad-brimmed hat entered the alleyway at the far end and strode directly towards her. Her heart pounded. Trapped between the two, she kept up her quickened pace but knew she had to face whatever was about to happen.

The boys were shouting at the tops of their voices, like hunters in for the kill, and the man ahead was racing towards her at an impossible speed. She froze. He came straight at her. She screamed. He shot past her without so much as a rush of air. The yells of triumph from behind turned to frantic screams of fear. The boys raced back along the alleyway as if pursued by a demon from Hell. Almost fainting, she staggered against the wall. When she finally recovered, the alleyway was deserted.

The world came back into focus, as if waking from a bad dream, but everything around her was real enough. A young couple entered the alleyway with a small child in a pushchair and smiled as they passed by. Slowly regaining confidence, she set off in the same direction towards the shops, aware she'd had a narrow escape that she didn't fully understand.

Reaching the town centre, she stopped at a coffee shop to fully recover herself. The lad from the warehouse had known she was going into town that afternoon because he'd commented on it in the restroom. She couldn't believe he'd go to such lengths with a gang of his mates. But hurt pride was apt to bring out extremes in some people, especially if they felt inadequate and publicly humiliated. She shuddered at what they might have done. She imagined being slashed with a knife as they cornered her and made a run for it. But what was the man in the coat doing there? He appeared just at the right moment, scaring them off. She realised he might have saved her from something she couldn't bear to think about. But why? And how? It didn't make sense. Instead of challenging him for watching her, she now felt grateful to him.

No longer in the mood to try on clothes, she wandered into a quieter part of town where there was a second-hand bookshop and a couple of junk-antique shops where occasionally she'd found a bargain. The pavements were less crowded there and so it surprised her to see the man in the long coat walking casually on the other side of the road and heading towards one of the shops. When she saw which one he entered, she determined to confront him.

A loud bell sounded as she entered the shop to be greeted by the musty smell of antiquity. Objects were piled high in no particular order: a doll's house, some straw hats, a letter rack, several books, a couple of old bottles and a stuffed raven were precariously perched on a long dusty dining table. Shelves of books and old magazines stood behind an ancient phonograph and some glass cabinets containing brooches, sets of cutlery and old keys, all randomly displayed.

She wandered deeper into the cavernous premises seeking the man in the coat but instead was greeted by a balding, middle-aged man who emerged from behind a curtain asking if he could help. She came straight to the point.

"I'm looking for a man I saw come in here just now. I want to speak to him."

"No, Miss, the bell didn't ring until you came in."

"But I saw him."

"I'd have heard the bell if anyone else had come in before you. It's been quiet all day."

"He was wearing a long overcoat and a broad-brimmed hat pulled down over his face."

"Aah, yes! I know who you mean. But he isn't here."

"You know him?" she asked with surprise.

"Yes, I know him. He comes in here sometimes but when he does, the bell never rings and I never know he's here until I hear him rummaging about. As soon as I hear him, I come into the shop but he's always gone by the time I get here and I see him through the window walking away down the street. So if he was here just now, he's done what he always does. Sometimes I just see him walking by, perhaps several times in a week, then I don't see him for months."

"But who is he?"

"A local man. He used to own this shop and when he sold it to my father he was most generous in lowering the price because he knew he was struggling to afford it."

"Well, I've seen him a lot in the past week," she explained. "I'm sure he's been watching me. But I've never seen his face. I only recognise him by his coat and hat."

"He's very self-conscious about his face. He was caught in a fire. Some say it was started deliberately. He was badly disfigured and he worried it would scare people. But I know from experience, he's a good man, not one to be frightened of. A real benefactor in this town. Outspoken about lots of things and always helping people."

"Where can I find him?"

"Oh, I doubt you can, Miss."

"Why not? You said you often see him passing by."

"I do. And you're not the first person to come in here asking about him. It's as if he leads people here so they can understand what's happening."

"What do you mean?"

"He can't stand injustice and always tries to intervene when he knows something bad is about to happen."

"That's exactly what he did this afternoon. But he's been watching me all week and it's scared me."

"If I understand the situation correctly, Miss, I'd say he was just looking out for you. Appearances aren't always what they seem. He wouldn't have wanted to you to see his face in case it frightened you. He has such a strong belief in protecting people and he said the one advantage of being disfigured is how he might use it to scare off anyone intent on violence or evil."

"But how does he know when someone is in danger?"

"Who knows? He's been dead and buried for thirty years or more. But who knows what can be seen from beyond the grave?

Dead he is, but he's never gone away. From what you tell me, he's done what he came to do. And you're not the first. I very much doubt you'll see him again, Miss."

That night before going to bed, she looked out from the window. There were still flecks of snow in the air but no one stood beneath the lamp. And the shopkeeper was right, she never saw him again.

THE LAKE IN THE WOODS

I thought I knew those woods very well. I'd walked there so often, sometimes when I needed to think about a specific problem or challenge, other times simply for the sheer pleasure of being surrounded by trees, listening to the birdsong and seeing the wildlife scurry about all around me. It was there that I discovered I could be invisible.

I was awake very early one morning and having had enough sleep, decided to go for a walk in my beloved woods. There was an autumn mist and the air had that distinctive smell of damp, fertile earth. Everything was fresh as if past events had been erased and that new dawn was the first day of all life. I was so enchanted by this sensation that I stopped in a clearing, completely motionless, listening, not wanting to make the faintest sound as I silently and slowly looked around me. After many minutes, my enchantment was magnified as, one by one, woodland creatures began cautiously emerging from the undergrowth and carried on as if I wasn't there. First a squirrel, then a woodland mouse, then a pair of rabbits less than a yard from where I stood. Robin, thrush, blackbird, magpie and crow all paid visits, seemingly oblivious of my presence until, to my astonishment and delight, even a young deer wandered into the clearing. By then I realised that my stillness had made me invisible. I don't recall how long it was that I stood just watching and listening but it felt as if I'd stumbled into another world, some kind of tranquil paradise. Finally, I moved, taking one step forward and, sensing my presence, every creature froze. The deer was the first to flee. Another step and the clearing was instantly deserted as I continued on my way, observed, I am sure, by countless cautious eyes. Suddenly the spell had been broken ~ paradise lost.

That experience prompted me to reflect on the very nature of paradise. What could it be? The more I considered, the more I thought that it could not be just one place. We will each have our own idea of what it is. There must be as many versions of paradise as there are people, just as there must be as many paths to eventual enlightenment as there are people. Could the two be the same? Is paradise enlightenment, or is enlightenment paradise? From that day on, I realised that I was on my own individual path through life that would, I hoped, one day lead to my own paradise.

As I said at the beginning, I thought I knew those woods perfectly well, until one day I arrived at a lake I'd never seen before. I must have mistakenly missed a familiar path and ventured unwittingly into a part of the wood, the existence of which was entirely unknown to me. It was a revelation and I was delighted to discover something new. This was about a year after that enchanted moment when I was invisible to the creatures around me, and during the intervening time I had often pondered the questions that that experience had raised about paradise. Nature ~ always a more profound teacher for me than any religion ~ posed so many questions. As for the lake, once I had discovered it, I revisited it on many occasions. Curiously, there were times when, despite being certain that I was on the right path, the way to the lake eluded me and I returned home disappointed. Perhaps that was because on those occasions I was too preoccupied with mundane matters to watch where I was going, but at other times I had no difficulty finding it.

On one particular day I sat peacefully beneath an ancient oak tree and gazed entranced at the beauty of that lake, so still and undisturbed with a solitary rock rising from its centre, upon which many a bird would briefly rest before flying off again. That rock reminded me of a temple garden in some distant eastern land where, instead of being surrounded by water, it would be a significant focal point amid a sea of meticulously raked sand. Far from spoiling the view of the lake, which otherwise would be like many others, it bestowed upon it a singular character that seemed to suggest some strange hidden meaning that preoccupied me.

Knowing the secret of invisibility, I sat without movement, breathing calmly the evocative scent of waterlilies, as I waited for that other world to reveal itself, which it always did, allowing me to observe and share its innocence and beauty as, one by one, many different creatures cautiously emerged from the surrounding cover. Often I had sat there for hours, even until the light began to fade, before making my way home.

And the light is fading again now as, once again, I sit beneath that familiar tree and a delicate crescent moon appears in a sky not yet dark enough to reveal the stars, and a distant owl calls out on this late summer evening. It is time for me to leave and yet I remain, confident of finding my way back through the woods in darkness. In contented tranquillity, as still as the tree against which I lean ~ as though I have become an integral and organic part of nature's own realm ~ I remain sitting, gazing at the lake.

Suddenly, there is a disturbance of water, a flurry of activity, a final splash and there, sitting on the rock is a most unexpected creature, wet and glistening, with its back towards me and, for all the world, looking like something almost human. The shock of its appearance stuns me. Not daring to move or make the slightest sound, I watch from where I sit while whatever it is seems completely preoccupied in some activity that I cannot see. As I wait, wondering whether it will move and reveal more of itself, my mind is filled with images I've seen in paintings of naiads, nymphs and mermaids, but this creature is like none of them. Its short, dark hair, still dripping water from the lake, is in contrast to its gamine, feminine figure. The lithe, glistening, slender back, so subtly fluid in every tiny movement, suggests something androgynous and other-worldly.

At its sudden emergence from the lake, several foraging creatures close by are startled and freeze into invisibility before suddenly darting for cover in the surrounding foliage. A fox that had been about to emerge into the evening light, instantly retreats the moment the creature appears and as the rustlings gradually subside, an unearthly silence falls upon this place. I must be the only living thing left exposed, watching in fascination as the being remains possessed by whatever it is doing that is still obscured from me.

Its head is bent slightly forward and its elbows make curious movements while its fluid spine moves at different angles in almost every direction, sometimes as if it is reaching down to gather up something from the water, while all the time remaining fully engaged with whatever it is doing. With its back still turned towards me, I could easily creep silently away but I am mesmerised by this fantastical being, like something from an ancient legend that I am privileged to witness. After a while, my curiosity becomes ever keener, not only to see this being from a better vantage point, but also to know precisely what it is that so engages its attention.

The reaction of all other life forms around me suggests that the creature on the rock is something to be feared, a predator, but that might simply be because of its size and human appearance, and that, in fact, it is no more a predator than I. Nevertheless, I am extremely cautious as I stand up and stretch my limbs, ready to steal, one very slow step at a time, around the edge of the lake in search of a better view and a clearer understanding of what this creature is.

A mixture of excited curiosity and an unnamed fear possess me as, in the encroaching dusk, I take my first tentative steps towards the lake. Keeping a safe distance from the edge, I trace a path that will allow me to see from a different angle this magical being, so engrossed in its activity. Not knowing for sure whether the creature has the same keen senses as other animals, I move as silently as possible, and as I pause between every cautious step, I see reflected in the lake, the crescent moon, lying mysteriously in the serenely still water directly behind the rock on which the creature sits. Almost afraid to glance in its direction, for fear of attracting its attention, I gradually gain a better view. The last thing I want is for it to be startled and disappear back into the water before I have a chance to observe it properly.

As I move silently closer, its attention remains focussed on some minutely detailed object that it appears to be constructing with the most delicate and refined movements of its slender hands. What I had thought of at first as androgynous now seems genderless, neither male nor female, despite features of the utmost delicacy and elegance. Suddenly it looks up. I freeze, hoping to become invisible. Turning to stare straight at me, its lizard tongue darts across the lake with unerring accuracy. I feel its saliva on my neck and I am paralysed.

Still standing and breathing, startled by its ability to reach me from such a distance, I am unable to move my limbs or turn my head while my gaze is now fixed in the direction of this mysterious being, which, having incapacitated me, returns its attention to whatever it is constructing. The image of that glistening creature sitting on the rock beneath the moon, like a sage in meditation, is forever seared into my mind, for I am forced to watch it, unable to move a muscle, until the stars appear one by one and dusk imperceptibly passes beyond the gates of total darkness. Only now does the creature complete its task and, reaching down, plucks a large flat leaf from a waterlily, upon which it places the object of its endeavours and propels it towards me across the mirrored water. At the same moment, quite miraculously, I find myself able to move again.

Immobilised for so long in the slowly encroaching darkness, my eyes have had all the time they need to become accustomed to whatever light remains and yet there is something else. The stars and the lunar crescent now seem brighter than I have ever known them and in the darkness I find myself able to see with complete clarity. Free to move, it doesn't even cross my mind to attempt an escape. Instead, I am mesmerised by the creature on the rock as it looks in my direction and points with a luminous slender arm towards the leaf that is floating towards me across water that is otherwise uncannily still.

As my gaze shifts back and forth between the rock and the leaf, the creature stands, elegant as a dancer, poised beneath the stars and glowing as if it has absorbed the light of the dying day, before making a cryptic sign and slipping noiselessly away beneath the water. I feel an unaccountable sadness at its departure for even though it exerted its power over me, it did not harm me. A moment later, the leaf reaches the shore and I lean down to retrieve the strange object.

Lifting it carefully, I hold in my hands a meticulously constructed labyrinth which, in turn, is enclosed within intricately woven strands that form what looks like a cage. It is an object of extraordinary beauty, a work of art, and I am in awe of its construction and the tireless patience that has been devoted to creating something so flawless. But it is also distinctly sinister. At the centre of the labyrinth is an effigy which, to my horror, I recognise as myself. I stare without comprehending, seeing myself helplessly trapped at the centre of a complex labyrinth, contained within a cage, as I wonder why it has been given to me and what it means.

If the effigy inside had not been so recognisable, I might simply have dismissed it as a clever construction and an accomplished piece of art, but it is plainly intended for me, which, in turn, seems to suggest that the creature had been aware of my presence all along. Of course, I have no way of knowing this, but why else would it have constructed this intricate, three-dimensional object containing my own effigy if I was not here to receive it? The closer I examine it with my mysteriously enhanced vision, the more it seems to me that this elaborate construction is, in fact, a message. And the longer I hold it in my hands, the more I feel a sense of suffocating confinement as if I have become the effigy trapped inside.

In panic and revulsion, I throw the object to the ground and grind it beneath my foot. For a fleeting moment the sense of confinement recedes but then quickly reasserts itself, as if in defiance of my action, and as it begins to take root, accompanied by a growing sense of panic and nausea, I am gripped with a desperate need to be free. In the midst of my turmoil, an intuitive awareness ignites in my mind and I begin to understand that in order to free myself from this sense of entrapment, it is necessary for me to release my own effigy from its labyrinthine prison.

Stung by this realisation and my own stupidity, instantly I remove my foot from the discarded object which, despite my attempt to destroy it, is not only undamaged, but unscathed in any way. Whatever it is made of is indestructible, a fact which, in itself, gives me cause for alarm. If I cannot free myself by destroying it, then my only other option is to solve the conundrum of my release. With the labyrinth once again cradled in my hands, I quickly find a place to sit as I fight against my sense of confinement, setting to work and focusing my mind on the task at hand. I begin by turning the construction at every angle to determine how it has been put together. Surely, whatever has been made can be unmade, even if it takes as long as the original process, but on first inspection the object seems impenetrable.

Scrutinising every detail with my unaccountably sharpened nocturnal vision, I search for any loose end that will give me a clue to dismantling what has been constructed. And it is precisely my enhanced vision that is the tool for my success. Even in the darkness I can see the minutiae of this object and I finally discover a single strand, caught in the dim starlight, that is the first key to my release. With hands so much clumsier than those used to construct it, I manage with difficulty to unwind that single thread which, in turn, leads to the next, and to the next, and to the next, until the outer cage is completely unravelled, giving me access to the labyrinth within.

This task takes all my concentration and I have become as engrossed as the creature was as it interwove every strand of what is, in truth, a prison. In my endeavour, I lose all sense of time and have no memory of changing my position at any moment during that laborious process. So focused and determined am I to achieve my goal and gain access to the labyrinth, that when finally I look up from my task, I am astonished to discover that I am sitting where the creature had sat, surrounded by water on the rock in the centre of the lake.

How I have been transported here is impossible to say but

the fact remains. Whatever enchantment is at work, I have no power over it, but I know that, with the outer cage now removed, my next task is to manoeuvre the effigy of myself through this complicated labyrinth in order to free it, and thereby free myself from this crushing sense of confinement. But as I set to work again, it soon becomes apparent that the water by which I am now surrounded provides another key to my success. The crescent moon, having changed its position over time, is now reflected directly in front of me and visible within the crescent is a conjunction of three stars that seem strangely familiar. As I shift my focus from the reflection back to the labyrinth, I can see an almost identical pattern echoed at its centre, that clearly suggests through which of several arches I must proceed to begin my journey towards the outer exit. The duplicated pattern from macrocosm to microcosm appears, for all the world, to be pointing the way to my release.

With judicious manipulation, I manage to manoeuvre the effigy through the chosen arch. Using all the delicacy and care I can muster, I continue to guide the figure along many convoluted passages, around sharply angled corners and intricate junctions, turning the labyrinth in the most precise and subtle ways to steer my imprisoned self towards what I desperately hope is my freedom. And so it is. My skill and patience are rewarded. As the effigy finally falls into my hand, all sense of my confinement evaporates.

In the same instant, night becomes broad daylight and from the rock in the lake where I sit, I see an altogether different landscape. Illuminated and glowing, it is a landscape I recognise, the one I have always imagined as my own personal paradise. Now all my senses are heightened and every detail of this vision is bathed in a sublimely soft light, like a dream come true. But can it be real, or is it only an illusion or a dream? Eventually I manage to tear my gaze from that breath-taking view and look down at my hands. They hold nothing. The labyrinth has vanished. I am free.

Remembering that I am sitting exactly where the creature sat when it constructed the labyrinth, I recall its paradoxical nature and ambiguity, neither male nor female. What it offered me was a conundrum that now seems equally paradoxical, because at the same time, it gave me the keys with which to solve it. My enhanced nocturnal vision enabled me to unravel the outer cage. My mysterious transportation to the rock in the lake enabled me to see the reflected stars and crescent moon which became the key to escaping the labyrinth. At first I had thought the seemingly impenetrable object with which I'd been presented was intended as a torment. I could have left it floating on the lake, never picking it up, and returned through the woods to the life I had always known. But instead, through curiosity or design, I had lifted it from the floating leaf and, in so doing, accepted it. What I first regarded as a torment, appears to have been a gift. The gift was the opportunity, through a rite of passage, to find freedom in my own personal paradise, now stretched out before me. These were my first thoughts as I released myself from the labyrinth.

But now, standing on the rock in the middle of the lake, I am beginning to wonder whether I have, after all, been elaborately tricked. While I can see my paradise on the far shore, I have no idea how to reach it. Perhaps, even now, I am being toyed with and tormented by some mischievous nature spirit, laughing at my predicament as I stand here, stranded like the perfect fool. My paradise appears within my grasp and yet I hesitate. Perhaps it is an illusion created to deceive me by a mysterious being of whom I know nothing. And I have no way of knowing how deep the lake is, nor what dangers it might conceal. I could be pulled beneath the surface to some eternal watery torment by the very creature who so enchanted me and knows me better than I know myself. If I have been tricked and deluded into thinking my paradise is attainable, then perhaps I deserve nothing less than to be consumed in the strangely serene waters of this uncharted place. Still I hesitate, locked between hope and fear. But finally I summon the courage to meet my fate and, bracing myself, I step from the rock to sink or swim. And that is when I discover I can walk on water.

THE PRISONER

For countless years the prisoner had sat gazing at the wall on the opposite side of his cell. The chain around his ankle prevented him from his desire of getting close enough to touch it. Nevertheless, he knew every crack and every individual stone of that wall and of those on either side, but he refused his captors the satisfaction of seeing him face the wall to which he was chained. He knew exactly how many links there were in his chain and he knew, without even turning around to look, exactly how they were fastened to the wall behind him. To taunt him, his cell door would sometimes be left open - not often, but sometimes. And he knew, or was sure, that it was seldom, if ever, locked.

He also knew that his food was imminently due. The door opened and the same cowled figure entered with a piece of bread and a cup of water. The figure stooped down and placed the food, ceremoniously, only just within the radius of his chain. Then it stood, and as it turned to leave the cell, the prisoner glimpsed the blind stare of the skull beneath the cowl. That day the figure chose to leave the door ajar and thus the prisoner knew it would stay until the same time the following day, when once again he would receive his bread and water.

The sight of the door left open was agonising. He had lost count of the number of occasions on which he had been tormented so. To endure this torture and retain his sanity, he had devised a way of distracting himself. He looked at the wall before him and began once again to count each of its stones and each of its cracks, before reaching behind him to count each of the links in his chain. Whenever he lost count, he forced himself to start again. And so now he counted every one of the nine thousand stones. He counted every one of the nine hundred cracks. And then, without looking, he counted the nineteen links in his chain, knowing, without ever turning to see, exactly how it was fastened to the wall behind him.

Then panic seized him. He clutched at the air beyond his chain. As the years of torment pressed in, he could bear it no more. In desperation, and for the first time since his imprisonment, he refused his food and turned his back on it. And his gaze alighted on an unfamiliar wall - the wall to which he was chained and which represented for him his humiliation. Always, for countless years, he had stood firm and denied his captors the pleasure of seeing him face that wall.

But as he looked, his gaze fell upon the means by which his chain was fastened to it - *not* as he had always "known". He walked towards the hook over which the last link of his chain was placed and, sobbing, he removed it and departed from his cell.

ABOUT THE AUTHOR

Richard Howard

Since childhood, I have been interested in ghost stories, whether factual or fictional, and I've always been drawn to that borderland separating this world from the world I believe we have come from and from where I believe we return.

My stories vary considerably in length and end when there's nothing more to say.

PRAISE FOR AUTHOR

I greatly admire Richard Howard as a very fine and original writer.

- ALAN HOVHANESS (COMPOSER)

He is a spiritual writer, one of rare integrity, and each story is a testimony to his own insight.

- CORAL GUEST (BOTANICAL ARTIST)

Beautifully written and most fascinating.

- COLIN WILSON (WRITER AND PHILOSOPHER)

Richard Howard's stories immerse you in a variety of settings and atmospheres: sometimes mysterious and fantastical; other times more every-day and contemporary. All will surprise, chill or warm you in one or more combinations.
The writing creates such clarity of description, it is no effort to conjure each scene in your mind. As you are carried along, (often with tension mounting) it's as if a melody is weaving its way, developing as it goes, creating a composition. The use of language is varied, rich,

inventive and intelligent. There is a welcome combination of excellent storytelling.

- KEVIN WAITE (REVIEW ON AMAZON)

I got so much pleasure from reading these stories. Each one was like an escape into another world for me and I eagerly followed the journeys of all protagonists with keen anticipation for the outcome; I love all the twists, the different characters and the variety of themes relating to the supernatural. Reading each story was like watching a film, as they're so visual. Many made my spine tingle, other made me smile at their hidden messages. I think the author did a magnificent job of creating different narrative moods and pacing the story telling to suit the plots and I know I'll return to these stories time and again. I highly recommend it.

- MONIQUE OTAI (REVIEW ON AMAZON OF 'TALES OF THE LOST')

BOOKS BY THIS AUTHOR

Strange Tales In Fiction And Fact

Twelve stories including ghosts, a vampire, a Christmas story, and uncanny scenarios in a variety of settings, concluding with an essay about the author's lifetime of odd experiences, some of which have inspired the stories in this book.

Tales Of The Lost

Tales of the Lost is Richard Howard's second book of short stories that bring us face to face with some very strange encounters and some unexpected twists along the way. Each story inhabits its own individual world and is told in a very direct style.

These new stories range from realms of complete fantasy to modern day settings. Some are ghost stories, others are just scary, and most have a twist in the tail. In each one there is a character who, in one way or another, is lost, hence Tales of the Lost. This book is available from my website www.richard-howard.com

Last Rites

When the Abbot of a remote monastery is prompted to search old manuscripts locked away in a vault, he discovers the distressing story of a monk from an earlier time that throws a significant light on work being carried out to expand the monastic premises. It is only when the story of the monk is fully revealed that he realises they face a crucial battle between darkness and light.

Stars And Crystals

'Stars and Crystals' takes place one Christmas when a boy called Simon, together with his parents, is visiting Granny in her large old Victorian house in the countryside. Late on Christmas Eve, too excited to sleep, he can't believe his eyes when he sees Santa Claus standing in the garden below his window and beckoning to him. In the morning, eager to unpack presents from his Christmas stocking, he finds an unusual package containing something he didn't ask for. As events unfold in a bustling household with Annie, the friendly cook, his inebriated Uncle Bartholomew, spiteful Cousin Sarah and Jack, the menacing stable hand, Simon discovers a gift from an unexpected source.

Storm Child

During a violent storm, a young girl, Eleanor, comes face to face with a strange boy, which changes her world in ways she couldn't have imagined. Offered an opportunity to escape her unhappy life, she must find both the courage and exactly the right moment to fulfil her wish.